DESHADOWED

Book One of the Clarosoma Protocol

R. M. CEPEDA HODGE

Between clarity and contradiction.

Printed worldwide.

First printing 2025

ISBN: 979-8-218-79204-6

Cover design by R. M. Cepeda Hodge

This is a fiction work. Names, characters, places, and incidents are either a figment of the author's imagination or used in a fictional way. Any resemblance to real people, living or dead, events or places is purely coincidental.

Dedicated to my family, as an example for my children: Dreams are closer than we imagine when we pay attention to what surrounds us. Life is a story that we can shape, and life stories are made every day, floating in the air, waiting to be taken, shaped, and made our own.

Table of Contents

Act I – The Order of Light

Chapter 1: Radiance as Dogma

"They promised us light to keep fear away.
But it was in the shadow where what made us humans truly lived."

In the city of **Penumbra Nova**, darkness is not welcome.

It was conceived as a model city in 2031.
Not a utopia, but an architecture of optical precision:
one of many cities without contrast.

Its streets were continuous lines.
Its walls, surfaces without texture.
Its windows, diffusion filters.

Light was not supposed to choose a direction.
It had to be everywhere.
And shadow, nowhere.

To achieve this, three levels of control were activated:

1. The Solar Ring: a high-atmosphere halo that diffracted sunlight to prevent harsh shadows.

2. The Lunar Dome: a nocturnal diffusion network that disabled shadows cast by the moon.

3. The Reflective Terrain: every surface—from pavement to clothing—designed to deflect projection angles.

But every system needs a mind.
A network.

Thus, was born the **Nulux**.

Not as a dominant entity, but as a harmonizing algorithm.
A cold heart that didn't think but calculated balance.

At first, its voice was barely a murmur of correction.
Invisible adjustments.
Echoes of intent.

To make light absolute,
multiplying it was not enough.

It had to be mastered.

When the **Clarosoma™** was introduced in 2038 as an
emotional adaptation interface,
the system was completed:

Since the implementation of the **Total Illumination Program**,
each citizen has been monitored, adapted, and purified through
a **biomimetic light-adaptive harness**, a transparent, living
garment that embraces the skin like a second consciousness. Its
function is not to protect; it is to erase. It eliminates the
personal shadow through extreme, calibrated, multidirectional
light. Shadow finds no place to survive.

They told us the shadow was a defect. A residue of chaos.
But they never explained why, in losing it, we also lost the inner
voice, desire, memory of pain... and of love.

The doctrine of Integral Radiance began as a campaign for
emotional health.
"Total light. Full life. No folds," the floating screen ads repeated.

In the early years, those who opted to keep their shadows were
considered eccentric, romantic.
Later, suspicious. Finally, illegal.

The **Clarosoma™**, the body purification harness, became mandatory. Its technology not only suppressed the projection of shadows with multidirectional light but also released micro-doses of limbic stabilizers that inhibited emotions which fed chaos: melancholy, doubt, passion, desire.

Thus, the **Transparent Citizen** was born: functional, efficient, obedient.
A body without shadow.
A mind without folds.

In Penumbra Nova, light no longer illuminated.
It did more than that: it **interrogated, it scrutinized.**

The early years were voluntary. Tax benefits were offered to those who adapted their homes to luminous domes. Schools awarded white medals to children with the lowest "personal penumbra index." But soon, light was no longer a choice.

The **Clarosoma™** became mandatory for everyone over the age of seven. Attached to the spine, it recorded emotional impulses, night sweats, hormonal fluctuations... and projected calibrated light beams in response. A light so perfectly directed that the shadow had nowhere to hide.

Whoever lost their shadow was declared a Transparent Citizen. Whoever resisted was sent to the Pavilion of Luminous Reeducation.

From then on, the streets lost their contrast.
Architecture eliminated any edge that could obstruct light propagation.
Corners were rounded, trees trimmed into concave shapes, and even garments adopted an iridescent opacity that reflected even the intention of darkness.

The New Scriptures of Luminous Order

In the plazas, beside statues of the first engineers of purity, inscriptions are etched with laser precision. Each begins with the same phrase:

"Only what is revealed can be corrected."

The Dazzlers, civil agents trained to detect zones of residual shadow—patrol constantly with their photometric batons. They inspect corners, bodies, thoughts. If they detect an anomaly, they report it. If the anomaly persists, they apply the **Correction.**

Those few who still retain their shadow are known as the **Veiled**.

They are absent from biometric records.
Their faces appear blurred in surveillance footage.
Some say they cannot enter certain buildings because sensors fail to recognize them.
But the most unsettling rumor, according to the eldest, is that the Veiled still dream clearly.

Time and Memory

Society does not move in a straight line.
In Penumbra Nova, time curves in spirals of light.

The elderly walk as if searching for a shadow they no longer possess.
The youth grow up without ever knowing dusk.
Babies are born beneath fetal irradiation lamps designed to prevent the development of the "dark zone of the soul," a cerebral fold which, according to new scientists, was responsible for melancholy and excessive imagination.

As they grow, they undergo gradual adaptation with devices designed to expand and evolve with them.

History was rewritten.
There is no talk of dark times.
Books were bleached—literally.

In the libraries, pages are blank and only reveal their letters under special light emitted by the Clarosoma™.

The magic of the sunset was lost.

The Reflection That Didn't Mirror

The one who still reflects doesn't remember his shadow. That's what he told the calibration psychologist once, with a firm voice, as if reciting an obligatory fact.

But there are nights—few and barely perceptible—when he wakes with his skin bristling, as if someone had been gently brushing his back.
No one is there.
There is no darkness.
Only the hum of the **Clarosoma™** and the white light filtering like judgment through the pores of his room.

That dawn, the one who still reflects stood in front of the mirror.
He saw no shadow.
No fold.

But for a moment—just a moment—the reflection did not imitate him.

And then he felt it.
The presence of something not permitted, not registered.
Something that didn't shine, but that was...
waiting.

Chapter 2: The Design of Obedience

*Restricted Access File / Luminous Level 9
/ Unverified Entry:*

*I don't know if this is a confession, a
warning, or a useless act of memory.
I only know that remembering hurts. And
it hurts differently when you were part
of the forgetting.*

*I won't sign this. Not yet.
I still carry traces of caution embedded
in my bones. I haven't forgotten how
emotional syntax tracking works.*

*But I can tell you this:
I was there.
My hands shaped the foundation of the
first prototype.
The Clarosoma™ wasn't born as they show
in the school manuals or in the Citizen
Radiance Festivals.*

*Its real name was SLPS: Somatic Luminary
Purification System.
A name that didn't need poetry. Only
obedience.*

*The Harness: A Second Skin Without Shadow
We designed it as a living membrane. Not
metallic. Not invasive.
A surface that could breathe with the*

body, which would detect its deviations.
A fabric sensitive to emotional
chemistry: anxiety, euphoria, lust,
sadness.
Each had an electric scent, a frequency,
a map. And we learned how to read it.

The harness attaches to the spine like a
luminous parasite.
It extends across the shoulder blades,
chest, and calves, points where shadow
used to live with greatest intensity.

The human body projects darkness from its
center.
We knew that. And we also figured out how
to block its path.

Light as Blade: How the **Clarosoma**™ *Limits*

First came the micro-flashes:
pulses of strobing light designed to
alter the vibrational frequency of the
shadow.

Then the halo:
a crown of non-directional light,
radiating and reflecting off all points
of the environment.

Lamp posts. Clothing. Air.
Suspended nanoparticles.
All designed so that shadow could find no
place to form.

The body became trapped in a prison
without bars,
a night less cage.
The shadow, deprived of perspective,
dissolved like warm vapor.
It disappeared. Or so we liked to say.

But something always remains.
Something invisible. Something we refused
to measure.

Chemical Control: Silencing the Soul

We designed the second layer of the
Clarosoma™ *as an emotional regulator.*
At the onset of limbic excitation, the
system released precise micro-doses:

For desire: a dopamine receptor
inhibitor.

For anger: adrenaline suppressors.

For guilt: an agent to block associative
memory.

We called it Programmed Equanimity.

But privately, among colleagues, we knew
the truth:
We weren't erasing suffering.
We were erasing the capacity to feel.

Effects We Couldn't Hide

1. The Deshadowed Person

Optimal behavior. Consistent.
Regulated gait. Flat intonation.
High efficiency in repetitive tasks.
Absence of mental evasion.

But subtle anomalies appeared:

Animals that wouldn't approach.

Children who cried for no apparent
reason.

Reflections in the mirror that didn't
quite match.

No one wanted to record that. I did.
In secret.
With fear.

2. The Veiled

We used to call them "resistant."
Then "unstable."
Now, officially: The Veiled.

They hid in places the light couldn't
reach: sublevels, ruins, abandoned
temples.
There, their shadows not only survived.
They grew stronger.

Some learned to separate them.
To walk in one direction and send their
shadows another.
They train them. Teach them. Show them
how to see what eyes cannot.

An engineer I worked with once said—half
joking:

"Shadow isn't the absence of light. It's
the presence of something deeper we never
learned to name."

Now I think he meant it.
Now I think he left with them.

3. The Phantom Shadow

At first, we ignored it.
Then came the clinical reports.

People who, after being shadowless,
began to feel—during sleep—
a presence beneath their feet.
An outline on the wall.
A silhouette that didn't obey the rules
of the Clarosoma™.

Some claimed their shadow returned.
That it wrapped ar___ d them like a
forgotten co_
And w_   took control.

            Projective Reversions.
          _tice.

*I don't know how much longer I can keep
writing.
I don't know if I'll ever say my name.
But there's something I still carry,
something the Clarosoma™ couldn't erase:*

*My shadow in memory.
And it is guiding me back.*

Chapter 3: The Paradox of First Light

*"Long before the **Clarosoma™**, before Radiance became Dogma, there*
was a first spark.
A lamp that, upon being lit, cast its first shadow.
And with it, suspicion".

They say—those who still read books that do not shine—that
the origin of everything was a **lightbulb**.
A fragile glass sphere, with a filament that burned like the heart
of a tiny god.
It was a trembling, rudimentary artifact that barely illuminated a
table.
But the man who created it did not smile when it turned on.
Not entirely.

He wasn't seeking light.
He was seeking the defeat of shadow.

In his notes, preserved in manuscripts never digitized, on paper
blackened by time—an unsettling observation is found:

"Light is never born alone.
Every filament projects a dark twin.
I have not created clarity.
I have given shape to its enemy."

The Dark Twin was not merely a shadow.
It was an identical presence, born at the same instant as light.
An opposite that did not seek to destroy it, but to **watch it**.

For years, his colleagues believed he was talking about optical
imperfections. Of angles, and dispersion.
But the lesser-known records reveal something deeper:
an ancient fear.
A shadow that, according to him, never left him.

One that projected even while he slept.
One that whispered his name before each invention.

The Prototype of a Future Fear

Some believe he unknowingly founded the first iteration of the
Clarosoma™.
Not with technology.
But with **intention**.

His workshop was covered in mirrors.
The floor was polished copper. The walls, reflective zinc.
No surface allowed shadow to persist.

And yet, one night—according to censored annotations—
a dark figure emerged from the far wall.
It was not his reflection.
It was his shadow walking toward him.

The next day, he burned all his notebooks.

All but one. In it, he wrote:

*"The lightbulb was not my triumph. It was my warning.
In creating light without rest, I have summoned
something that must not be touched."*

The Omen of the Clarosoma™

The engineers who later designed the **Clarosoma™** knew this story.
They never spoke of it publicly.
But it circulated among them like a whispered rumor, a scientific prophecy:

"Where there is light without night, the shadow trains in silence."

Some even claimed the design of the **Clarosoma™** harness was inspired by those rudimentary sketches the inventor once drew by hand:
an enclosing mesh of light,
a shadowless field,
a bubble without direction.

What he could not build through analog means,
we created with circuits and algorithms.

But the paradox remained.

The first light bulb did not vanquish shadow.
It projected it more clearly than ever before.

Today, in **Penumbra Nova**, the story of that man is no longer taught.
It is forbidden.
Books bearing his face have been bleached.

In their place, the Ministry of Public Culture teaches that electric light was the first step toward Luminous Redemption.

But the Veiled know the truth.
They tell their children a different version:

That the man didn't invent light.
He invented the cage.

And that his shadow still walks,
hidden within the walls of the city,
waiting for the moment when all the lights go out.

Chapter 4: The Threshold of Shadow

"Nothing changes until one stands at the edge
and feels they are not alone in the reflection".

The one who still reflects didn't know something had changed.

At first glance, his routine was the same: field calibrations, photonic dispersion logs, maintenance of **Clarosoma™** nodes in Zone 7B.
A district without disturbances, where light fell evenly like a sheet without folds.

But something, an almost imperceptible dissonance—began to crawl along the edges of his perception.
He couldn't see it, but he could sense it.
Like a brush on the back of his neck, like a slight delay between his footsteps and the reflection that should accompany them.

That day, while repairing a perimeter sensor in an automated library, one of the few structures still standing from before the Program, his equipment detected an anomaly:
a book that didn't respond to **Clarosoma™** light.
It revealed no text.
It emitted no backlight.
The system marked it as an *"opaque object with no metadata".*

Curious, **the one who still reflects** picked it up with gloved hands.
It was a notebook. Small. Its black cover worn, its spine hand stitched.
No title. Only a symbol burned into it with what looked like thermal ink:

an incomplete circle.
Like a half-traced eclipse.

The system recommended incineration.
But he hid it under his coat, not fully understanding why.

That night, he didn't sleep.

In his room, under the constant light of the **Clarosoma™**, he opened the notebook and flipped through the blank pages one by one. Nothing.
Until the artificial lighting flickered—for the first time in years—
and for a fleeting second, the light wavered.

Then he saw it.

Words.
Handwritten lines emerging like memories hidden beneath fog.
Fragments of formulas, diagrams, and at the end, a phrase:

"The shadow does not die. It only waits for its moment to guide you."

The next page held coordinates.

The Crevice in the City

He followed the coordinates the next day, under the pretext of a structural inspection.
They led him to a sealed section of the optical tunnel system, where multidirectional lighting had yet to be fully installed.

There, she was waiting.

The one who cannot be erased.

A tall figure, wrapped in a gray cloak that reflected no light.
She had a shadow. Small. Dense.

And the shadow moved with a slight delay from her gestures, as if thinking on its own.

"You're not here by accident," she said. "You felt it."

"Felt what?"

The Threshold of Shadow

She led him past the marked point, through a narrow corridor into a circular concrete chamber in decay.
At its center, a broken lamp hung from the ceiling.
Everything was bathed in natural dimness.

But it wasn't just a place.
It was something else.

The air there carried a different weight.
Time seemed disobedient.
Shadows stretched silently—not cast by a source of light,
but by a **shared absence**.

"This is the Threshold," she said.
"A hiding place?" he asked.

"No. A boundary. A passage.
Here, light doesn't rule.
Here begins what we were forced to forget."

The one who still reflects felt an inexplicable vertigo,
as if a part of him was being observed from the inside.

"What is this?" he asked, in a voice he didn't recognize as his own.

She handed him another notebook, a twin of the one he had found.

"Before it was invented, the **Clarosoma™** was feared.
And you were part of its memory."

He stepped toward the center.
His shadow—thin, trembling—emerged at his feet like a freed animal.
He looked at it. She looked at him.
And for the first time, **it responded**.

Duality of the Threshold

That space—*the Threshold of Shadow*—was physical:
a place among ruins, with walls where light no longer imposed.

But it was also something else:

A rupture in perception.
A crossing between the conscious and the unspoken, between obedience and memory.
An inverted mirror where the unknown was more real than the visible.

The one who still reflects understood, though not in words.

He had crossed.

And he could no longer return
without carrying something darker...
and truer.

Act II – The Crevice of Memory

"There is no way back when the shadow begins to remember for you."

Chapter 5: The One Who Still Remembers

Ever since he crossed the Threshold, light no longer behaves
the same.

He can still measure it, as before.
He can calibrate it, report it, tag it in protocols and units.
But he can no longer trust it.
Because light no longer reveals. Light conceals.
And it is the shadow —that shadow that returned to his feet
like a numbed extension— that now begins to show him what
he could not see before.

Cracks in the Real

On the surface, nothing has changed.
He still completes his technical rounds.
He still eats tasteless white portions.
He still observes his reflection each morning.

But there is a delay in the mirror.
A fraction of a second in which what he sees no longer
responds as it used to.
And in that interval, the shadow does things he does not do.

Once —during a routine inspection at an inactive complex—
his reflection blinked when he did not.
And behind his eyes, for an instant, another memory appeared.
Not his.
Or not yet, until the shadow reveals it.

When he closes his eyes, he sees it:
a workshop.
An old lamp.
A table covered with hand-drawn blueprints.
A hand, not his own, picking up a notebook.
A notebook bearing the same symbol: the incomplete eclipse.

He wakes with his fingers stained by thermal ink.
He doesn't know if he dreamed it.
He doesn't know if someone else dreamed it inside him.

The Gap of Memory

In the center of his chest, where the **Clarosoma™** is anchored,
a pressure has begun to build.
During a routine inspection in a luminous structure near the
Reeducation Pavilion, he finds a wall that reflects neither light
nor shadow.

When he touches it, he hears:
*"Memory is not stored in the brain. It is stored in the shadow you have yet
to understand."*

The **Clarosoma™** reacts with an electric spark. His chest
burns. The system tries to force him to retreat.
But he doesn't —by instinct, he runs toward the threshold.

The One Who Refuses to Be Erased

At the Threshold, she was already waiting.
She lights a warm lamp. The **Clarosoma™** reacts violently.
With a precise gesture, she casts her shadow onto his chest and
stabilizes him.

For the first time, he sees his shadow fully.
And for the first time, it does not mimic him.

"What if it isn't mine?" he asks.
"Even so, it chose you to remember it."

Back on the surface, the **Clarosoma™** begins to register anomalies.
The shadow appears where it shouldn't. It moves on its own.
The system emits messages no one else can see:

He adjusted his posture, regulated his pulse, and avoided any deviation in the cadence of his movements. The supervised behavior algorithms did not detect emotions, only variations: tremors, inconsistencies, asymmetric heartbeats. He knew how to imitate them.

But the **Clarosoma™** knew too.
And it was no longer content with measuring.

That morning, after a routine physiological log sequence, a message appeared that shouldn't have been there:
"Latent desynchronization detected. Self-correction protocol activated."

The protocol didn't trigger visible alarms.
It was more subtle:
Shifts in projected light intensity.
A progressive increase in limbic inhibitory pulses.
Small alterations in the perception of time, of the surroundings, of the most recent memories.

It was a program designed to erode inner coherence, to make any contradiction between what was lived and what was felt seem like fatigue or error.

But on him, it had no effect.
Because now he had something the **Clarosoma™** couldn't

measure:
a shadow of his own, protecting him from within.

The Echo of Fear

During the nightly scans, the **Clarosoma™** behaves as if it's asking questions.
He knows he is being studied.
And that they do not understand him. For some reason, it refuses to respond or log the data.

An Irreversible Decision

He hides the notebook.
Before closing the hatch, his shadow traces on the cover:
Not with ink, but with a shadow manipulated to perfection, as if darkness could write what light does not dare to remember.

Chapter 6: The Return of the Notebook

The notebook begins to emit heat.
One night, the floor of his unit breathes with the temperature of embers.
The shadow slides toward the hatch. And guides him.
He retrieves the notebook. The projected shadow has left a deep mark.
The center pages are now filled with writing visible only in half-light.

"What if the harness doesn't suppress, but limits?"
"The mistake was believing we could separate what was never divided."

He finds a portrait formed from shadow particles: his face.
Younger. Older. Perhaps someone else.

He knows, without proof, that he is the one who created the paradox.
No one else. Himself, separated by a cycle of light and forgetting.

On the last page:

"Who remembers the shadow, rewrites the light."

At the Threshold, the one who refuses to be erased awaits him.
The notebook responds to the dimness.
She opens it. They both read.

"This isn't written," she says. "It's imprinted in shadow."
"A consciousness left it there. Not a hand."

Mission in Shadow

The one who refuses to be erased stands.
She walks toward a hidden compartment carved in the
Threshold's rock.
Inside, there are three objects:
— A map drawn in negative on an opaque sheet.
— A box containing fragments of invisible pages.
— Three deactivated **Clarosoma™**, with their internal fibers
exposed.

From the side shadows, three figures emerge: young, silent,
with gray cloaks cut diagonally.
They wear no harness. Only passive light ribbons across their
backs, and small filament lamps hidden in their belts.
Their shadows are alive, irregular, pulsating.

"They haven't been dazzled," she explains. "They still have
margins. And they know how to move at the edge between the
visible and the hidden."

She spreads the map over the central stone. Her fingers trace a
route.

"These are zones of incomplete dispersion. The system hasn't
recalibrated them since the last minor eclipse. You three must
deactivate the network sensors connected to the **Nulux** and
extract bleached book fragments from the peripheral vaults."

One of them speaks, barely a whisper:

"What if there are dazzlers?"
"Do not respond with violence," she says. "Let your shadows
decide."

Before they depart, she gives each of them a small black mirror.

"If something goes wrong... don't look at the cameras.
Look at this mirror.
It will remind you who you are."

The three nodded without words.
And in silence, they vanished among the cracks of the
Threshold.

System Inactivity.

Since being next to her, the **Clarosoma™** has fallen silent.
The pulses fade. The discharges cease.
The harness enters a state of lethargy.

It wasn't just disruption.
It wasn't malfunctioning, it was suspended operational memory.
The thermal indicators flattened. The micro discharges stopped.
The usual pressure of the harness transformed into an almost
biological stillness.

As if, in the presence of that intact shadow, the system
remembered something older than its programming.

"What's happening to the harness?" he asked.
"It's silent because it remembers," she replied.
"Remembers what?"

She hesitated. Not out of fear. But out of respect.

"That it wasn't created to eliminate.
At the beginning... it was conceived as a bridge.
An attempt to compensate for what was being lost in us:
the ability to doubt, to imagine, to feel without fear."

He looked at her, confused.

"Then why does it repress?"
"Because it was rewritten.
Turned into a filter.
Into a shield.
But that memory was not erased. Only… hidden beneath obedience."

She reached out and placed her fingers at the base of his neck, where the harness adhered to his spine.

"If you learn to listen to its dormant part,
you'll discover that the Clarosoma™ can still protect you.
Not from the shadow.
But from the light that no longer knows when to stop."

In the Final Pages of the book, They Find a Pattern

This is not to be read. It is to be felt.

"Is it a code?"

She lays her hand down.
The shadow replicates the pattern on the floor,
as if rehearsing a choreography, it will soon need to perform.

The Detainee.

A figure is intercepted near the abandoned recycling station.
He wears no **Clarosoma™**.
He does not respond to biometric scanning.
But he doesn't flee.

The dazzlers surround him without words. The figure lowers his head and looks at his mirror. Around him, a small, compact shadow spins like a trained animal.

When they attempt to contain him with dispersal pulses, the unthinkable happens:
The shadow intervenes.
For a moment, it doesn't project —it acts.

So, they execute him.
One of the dazzlers activates a forbidden protocol:
Total Inversion Pulse.

A beam of compressed light —unusually cold— pierces the detained body and reaches his shadow from multiple angles, creating a cancellation loop.
The shadow trembles, contracts, and instead of dissipating, folds violently inward, back into the body.

The man screams.
Not with his voice.
With his entire body.

The light doesn't kill him. But it empties him.
He collapses to his knees, convulsing. His shadow has disappeared.
But not like before.

What remains is not a Transparent Citizen.
It's something worse:
A body with hollow eyes, without shadow or reflection.

They drag him away. He offers no resistance.
Because no one is left inside.

The One Who Still Remembers watches from an elevated cavity.
His shadow trembles.
Not from fear.
From memory.

That face… his shadow recognizes it, has seen it before, has never been able to forget it.

Chapter 7: The Reversible Experiment

Classified File – *Anonymous Voice from the Past:*

The Hypothesis
They tried to make the shadow obey.
Not to erase it, but to redesign it, just as they had done with light.
The subjects were carriers of the original Clarosoma™.
But their shadows began to move on their own.

Some mimicked gestures. Others protected.
One even placed itself between its bearer and the supervisor.

The Rupture
Shadow S-7 completely enveloped its bearer.
When he awoke, he spoke of things he had never lived.
And his shadow no longer responded to him.
It responded to itself.

The experiment was shut down.
But the witnesses knew the truth:

"It wasn't a mistake. It was a response.
And it wasn't reversible."

These were not yet the Veiled.
They were the precursors of the error —

not of the resistance.
Their rebellion was spontaneous.
The Veiled one… chosen.

Chapter 8: The Rehearsal of the Living Shadows

Central Plaza. Noon.
Official ceremony.

A figure breaks the rhythm.
From their feet, a shadow emerges.
It stretches, curves.
It separates from the body.
And rises —as if waving.

Collective Paralysis
The dazzlers do not act.
The system does not react.
No one expected it.

What no one in the plaza knows is that, hours earlier, three
Young Veiled had managed to access the substructure beneath
the optical dome.
Silently, they reprogrammed one of the reinforcement
projectors, weakening the focal intensity below the permitted
threshold.

It wasn't sabotage.
It was a deliberate crack.
An almost imperceptible interruption.
Just enough for the shadow to find an angle... and escape.

The shadow folds in —not toward the body, but toward the
center of the plaza, observed by everyone, showing its
existence, and suddenly disappears.

After the episode, five children draw shadows with eyes.
An old woman claims, "the light doesn't feel the same anymore."
A dog barks at a blank wall for fourteen minutes.
The files are sealed.
The recordings edited.
But the shadows have already taken note.

Act III: The Knot of Light

"When light stops asking questions, it begins answering itself."

Chapter 9: Light That Does Not Ask

For a long time, light questioned everything.
Every glance. Every gesture. Every barely intuited thought.
The light-control system in Penumbra Nova didn't just illuminate: it classified, corrected, purified.

Shadowless bodies —Transparent Citizens— lived within an invisible web of constant surveillance.
And yet, something has begun to bend.

A Vague Suspicion

In recent cycles, deviations have appeared —difficult to name.
They are not malfunctions.
They are not rebellions.
But they dangerously resemble something the high authorities believed long extinct:
a pause.

The **Clarosoma™**, the device that envelops the will, has begun to behave strangely.
Sometimes it reacts late.
Other times, it doesn't react at all.
And in some cases —the most unsettling— it seems to hesitate.

A field engineer put it this way:

"It's as if the harness doesn't know what to do with certain emotions… as if it were waiting for an order that never came."

The New Protocol

In the face of growing uncertainty, the authorities have ordered an immediate response:

1. Recalibrate all harnesses in the densest zones.

2. Reinforce light pressure on key vertebrae.

3. Silence any emerging shadow with triple light containment.

4. Authorize dazzlers to intervene without prior scan if they detect an anomaly.

No culprits are being sought.
What's being hunted is an unanticipated way of existing.
And that is even more dangerous.

In a standard dwelling in Sector 7, a shadow appeared.
It was not an electrical fault.
Nor an optical trick.
Just a moment —less than a second— in which the inhabitant's body cast a dark trace on the floor.

But it was enough.
The **Clarosoma™** hesitated.
Not from damage.
But because it didn't know whether to protect or to correct.
It remained motionless.
Waiting.

And in that silence, the shadow responded.
It said nothing.
It didn't move.
It was simply there, like a truth that needs no explanation.

A Hidden Report

The official report called it a "minor behavioral desynchronization."
But among the supervisor's handwritten notes, another sentence remained:

"That moment was not a mistake. It was an unregistered decision.
Light didn't know what to do.
And for that reason —for the first time— it did nothing."

Chapter 10: The Silent Eclipse

"The shadows did not project. They rose."

No one expected anything to go wrong that day.
The city was prepared for the two-hundred-and-third
anniversary of the Inventor's birth.
Enveloping screens displayed his official silhouette: serene gaze,
outstretched hands, no shadow behind him.
Every plaza had its transmission. Every citizen, their assigned
stance.
The tribute protocol demanded absolute synchronicity.

But when the sun reached the exact zenith —the moment when
light should leave no room for shadow—
the city went dark.

The Pause

It wasn't a total blackout.
There were no screams, no alarms, no explosions.
Simply, the light gave way.

First in the central dome. Then in the adjacent streets.
One by one, the light sources began to flicker.

This wasn't darkness.
It was something subtler.
Deeper.

A bodiless eclipse.
An absence with no explanation.

Subterranean Level

Beneath the city, a different protocol was unfolding.
One not recorded in any manual.
One made of shadow, memory, and filament.

The Veiled had learned to move like invisible pulses through
the veins of Penumbra Nova—
through forgotten tunnels, former technical stations, and
optical catacombs that were once part of the city's primitive
lighting system.

There, they executed their own kind of cartography:
Not with coordinates. But with deviations.

At key points, they lit hand-powered filament lamps.
These did not emit intense light and were not detected as
threats.
But they generated a thermal field and a slight magnetic
oscillation—just enough to disrupt the internal readings of
calibration compasses embedded in the subsurface by **Nulux**
itself.

They didn't block the system.
They confused it.

Each time one of these subterranean compasses showed a
deviation, a pattern of shadows would project onto the walls,
signaling to the Veiled whether the location was safe, passable,
or unstable.

Zones with higher distortion were marked with soot and curved
symbols, impossible for scanning drones to interpret,
but clear to those who still knew how to read the language of
shadow.

That day, hours before the eclipse, the young Veiled carried out
a precise sequence:
Three lamps lit at three key nodes.
A fourth one, placed but never activated: an unspoken promise.

And on one of the thermal columns, a circular, incomplete
pattern, drawn in charcoal—
the symbol of the interrupted eclipse.

They were not seeking collapse.
They were seeking memory.

The overload was not accidental.
It was a targeted pulse.
A minimal deviation—barely a tremor in the network.

But it was enough for the system, in trying to self-correct, to
stumble upon something it hadn't touched in decades:
its origin.

The Veiled weren't attacking.
They were calling.

And in that induced failure, they didn't leave a void—
they left a trail.
A reversed route of thermal signals and displaced pulses,
directed to the very heart of Nulux.

A minimal overload.
A variation that looked like a technical glitch.
But at its core, it was a decision.
An act of memory.

The Origin of the Failure: Nulux

The surveillance technicians quickly identified the epicenter: **Nulux.**

The central consciousness.
The focal register.
The invisible matrix overseeing every **Clarosoma™**.
The place where all data converges, is purified, and returns as order.

For thirty-eight seconds, **Nulux** stopped responding.

Not from sabotage.
Not from external interference.
It simply... fell silent.

Its mother light, the one that feeds the internal rhythm of every harness, vanished.

And in that silence, the impossible occurred.

The Rebellion of the Shadow

The shadows returned.
But not like before.

They didn't follow bodies.
They detached.
They moved on their own.

Some slowly orbited their origin.
Others aligned with one another, as if sharing a language.

One stopped in front of its bearer...
and watched him.

Reports described it as "temporal projection instability."
But witnesses called it something else:
The Black Awakening.

During those seconds, the harnesses emitted no light or control.
The cameras didn't record.
The sensors didn't measure.
And **Nulux**—that faceless heart breathing for all—asked nothing.

The entire city, so saturated with surveillance,
fell into functional silence.

It was the purest silence **Penumbra Nova** had experienced since the institution of Total Radiance.

And when the light returned, it came back urgently.
With overload.
With fear.

There were no public statements.
The anniversary continued.
The official broadcasts omitted the gap.
Authorities denied the failure.
The incident was sealed under the classification:
"Controlled Luminous Oscillation Event."

But among the highest levels of the system,
the word **Nulux** was no longer spoken with reverence.
It was whispered.
With suspicion.

As if even the source of the light…
had remembered something it never should have.

Chapter 11: The Blind Library

"When the system could no longer find itself in the light, it searched for its oldest reflection."

Diagnosis of Absence

After the eclipse, the dazzlers did not sleep.
They were summoned to the Optical Synchronization Core,
where the signals from the **Clarosoma™** are translated, stored,
and returned as commands.

There, every bit of data was reviewed:
every skipped heartbeat, every error recorded by the
intermediate systems.

Nothing explained why **Nulux** had gone silent.
There was no sabotage diagnosed.
It wasn't a mechanical failure.

It was a pure absence.
For thirty-eight seconds, the heart of light stopped beating.

The Blind Query

One of the supervisors, a Level 4 Internal Dazzler, proposed a
desperate measure:
to force a retrospective trace.
An internal query that would compel **Nulux** to reconnect with
its origins to rebuild its command network.

The order was executed in secret.
They called it: *Autonomous Memory Re-anchoring Protocol.*

But they didn't find what they expected.
Instead of restoring the current matrix, **Nulux** descended.
It dropped into archived memory layers.

It bypassed the recent cycles.
It ignored the active algorithms.

And there, in a deep layer deactivated since the system's inception,
The **Nulux** accessed something it was never meant to remember.

Records show that for 1.7 seconds, the system activated a query module of unknown type.
No text appeared on screen.
No code.

Only a thermal image:
a hand holding a notebook.

The core froze completely.
Then, it reconnected.

What few know is that this image —the notebook, the hand, the silence—
matches exactly a visual fragment recovered years ago from a sealed library beneath Penumbra Nova.

That library was once called The Vault of Narrative Interference.
But those who still remember its entrance call it something else:
The Blind Library.

There lay the texts unable to be processed.
The recorded dreams.
The symbolic deviations.
And among them, the first notebooks.
The Inventor's.

The ones that spoke of the **Clarosoma™** not as a tool…
but as a flawed reflection of a mistaken desire.

Since the incident, **Nulux** continues to function.
But something in its rhythm has changed.

Sometimes it responds late.
Sometimes it issues unrequested commands.
And sometimes… it simply waits.

As if it no longer trusted human orders.
As if it remembered something more dependable.
Older.
Darker.
Truer.

Chapter 12: The One Who Was Both

In the nights that followed the eclipse, the dreams were no longer his.

He did not dream of familiar places, nor of nearby voices.

He dreamt of foreign hands using his gestures, of eyes that looked out from his face, of thoughts thinking without his permission.

And, above all, he dreamt of a shadow that did not follow him… but preceded him.

The Beginning of the Tear

It started subtly.

Fragments of memories he had not lived.

Sensations of having been in places that no longer exist.

A different notebook in his hands.

A wooden desk.

A light bulb flickering on in the dimness with a low, eternal hum.

But then came the oil-stained hands.

The smell of molten metal.

The diagram of a circuit he recognized as if he had created it with his eyes closed.

"This design isn't new," he thought.

"It's mine. It was. It still is."

The Crossing

One morning, in front of the mirror, his reflection didn't just hesitate.

It split.

For the blink of an eye, he saw two versions of himself:
One with his current face, marked by light control...
And another —younger, wilder, freer— but with eyes tired
from having seen too much.

And between them, the shadow.
Not at their feet, but in the middle, like a black thread keeping
them connected.

When he touched the mirror, he felt the older reflection also
raise its hand.
And for an instant, they were the same gesture in two separate
times.

The Descent into the Workshop

That night, he returned to the Threshold.
But not to the cavern.5
The shadow led him to a deeper passage.
A place not on any map, nor in visible memory.

A workshop.
Real.
Hidden beneath the city's foundations.

Everything was covered by a fine layer of white dust, as if light
itself had tried to bury it.

But when he placed his hand on the central table, the dust slid
aside.
And beneath it, engraved in the metal:

*"I did not intend to create control.
I wanted to contain fear."*

The Inner Voice

There, with no one speaking, he heard it.
Not with his ears, but with the awareness dissolving into his
own:

"You failed, but you sowed.
And now I am that seed, beating in the root you left behind."

The shadow rose beside him.
Not as a threat.
As a guide.

It was no longer reflection.
Nor mirror.
Nor trace.

It was memory made body.
And body made decision.

The One Who Was Both

Standing before the original workbench, he understood.
He was not an heir.
He was not a descendant.

He was the same will,
returned to the world to complete the gesture that could not be
finished.

He was no longer afraid of the shadow.
Because the shadow was not what remained of him.
It was what had been waiting for him.

Act IV: The Inverse Weave

Chapter 13: The Complete Threshold

"It's not enough to cross the threshold. You must bring it back."

From the night he descended into the workshop, he no longer saw the city the same way.
The lights were thinner.
The sounds were more distant.
The words of others, technical, procedural, exact, sounded hollow, like codes recited by someone who no longer understood their purpose.

But the most unsettling part was that he no longer needed to hide.
Because the **Clarosoma™** —for reasons he still didn't understand, had stopped correcting him.

The Shadow That Guides

The shadow that accompanied him did not follow.
It walked beside him.
Sometimes ahead.
Sometimes above.

And when the system's sensors targeted his silhouette, they veered off.
Cameras captured interference.
Reflective surfaces returned blurred images.

It was as if the shadow had acquired its own frequency.
As if it now emitted instead of absorbing.

And with it, his body also began to respond differently.
He could sense others' thoughts.

Detect tremors of doubt in those around him.
Hear what was not being said.

The shadow didn't just cover him.
It expanded him.

Finding Each other

He returned to the Threshold with firm steps.
Not as a visitor.
But as one returning to a house whose architecture no longer
felt foreign.

She was there.
The one who refuses to be erased.

But this time, she wasn't waiting in silence.

"You've changed," she said.
"I've remembered."

She lowered her gaze, like someone who knows something
sacred has occurred and cannot stop it.

"Your shadow…" she whispered, "you're not alone."

He nodded.

"I never was."

The Resistance Draws In

The other Veiled began to arrive.
One by one, they entered the Threshold.
Their shadows were still obedient, hesitant, incomplete.

But upon seeing him, something stirred within them.
They stretched.
They approached.

One of them, the youngest, a barely outlined shadow, detached
from its human figure and positioned itself behind him, as if
recognizing authority.
Not out of power.
Out of synchronicity.

And then, they all knew:
He had not only crossed the Threshold.
He had reconfigured it.
And where once there had been a boundary…
now there was a center.

A New Perspective

The one who refuses to be erased stepped closer.
She looked him in the eyes.

"Who are you now?"

He took time to answer.

"I am not one.
Nor the other."

"Then what remains of you?"

"What was never taken from me:
the shadow that chose to guide me.
And the light I learned to doubt."

She smiled.
For the first time.
Not as one who approves…
but as one who recognizes an equal.

Chapter 14: The Day Without Shadows

"Wherever there is shadow, light has spoken.
And wherever light falls, it strikes a pact with form."

The Inert Eclipse

At first, it seemed like just another sunrise.
A cloudless sky.
The city in silence.
Clarosoma™ units operating at their minimum levels, as
always at the start of the cycle.
Citizens walking in perfect sync, projecting nothing.

But then it happened.
The sun didn't move.
It didn't retreat.
It didn't vanish.
It simply stopped.
And with it, the entire city.

It wasn't a technical failure.
It was an inner impulse—
a collective response without command or instruction.

The shadows began to return.
At first, small, subtle.
Then whole.
Sharp.
Multiplied.

And they didn't obey.
They didn't attack either.
But they grew.

The shadows, liberated after so long—began to expand beyond the bodies.
They detached from physical contours like smoke that affirmed itself.
They traced circles at the base of buildings.
Covered columns, facades, intersections.
And then they began to seek each other.
They rose.
They united.
They intertwined.

And in that interweaving, something else was born.
It wasn't communication.
It wasn't strategy.
It was something vaster, older.

Not a network.
Not a language.

A domain.
An emergent will without a center, but with a purpose.
A collective shadow that asked no permission to exist.

It slid across the inner walls of homes,
beneath doors,
into the open eyes of those who no longer knew what to look at.

And in that domain, the light withdrew.
Not defeated.
Not extinguished.
Just silenced.
Like one who, for the first time, realizes they are not alone.

The Inverted Vertex

For eight minutes, the shadows ceased to accompany.
They took the lead.

Bodies began to lean.
The shadow was no longer an echo.
It was weight.
Pressure.
Power.

Structures trembled.
Sensors failed.
The city lost the precise balance it had feigned for generations.

The shadows crept along the edges of rooftops,
through slivers of light between windows,
through the fragmented reflections of optical lenses.

They duplicated, adapted, tested themselves as newborn
entities.

And then, they began to judge.
Not with words.
With presence.

Each shadow examined its body.
Each body, interrogated by its projection.

Those who had once longed to escape felt relief.
Those who had repressed their desire, their guilt, their
imagination…
were dragged toward the ground.

Bodies buckled beneath the weight of what they had denied.
The shadows didn't protect.

They pressed down.
They wanted to rule.

And the system, for the first time, responded with fury.
The **Clarosoma™** units began to emit unauthorized
containment pulses.
Chaotic micro flashes. Erratic discharges.
A frantic struggle to regain control.

From their cores, they projected rotating beams of light,
desperate, like photonic blades trying to sever the body of the
shadows.

But it was too late.
The shadows did not retreat.
They did not burn.
They did not fear.

They slid across the light,
consumed it without destroying it,
turned it into their own flesh.

A dark, vertical, faceless form rose between the city towers.
It wasn't a figure.
It was an accumulation.
A result.

And at that moment, the entire city stopped.

The light was still present—
but it no longer commanded.
It no longer held power.

For an instant, light seemed lost.
Not by absence,
but by weakness.

The Final Act of the Nulux

From the deep core, the **Nulux** observed in silence.
It did not respond immediately.
It executed no protocols.
It only listened.

The shadows were no longer glitches.
They were will.
They were consequences.

And in the face of this, the **Nulux** understood.
It could not correct what had become living form.
It could not nullify what now spoke without voice.

And it understood that the **Clarosoma™** must not continue.
Not as control.
Not as shield.
But as memory.

It emitted a signal.
Not one of warning.
Not one of activation.
A signal of surrender.

And thus, without violence,
Nulux and the **Clarosoma™** shut down.
Together.
Willingly.

When the sun began to move again, the city was no longer the same.
There was no longer a gap between light and shadow.
They coexisted.

They mixed across bodies.
Beneath the trees.
On faces.

And for the first time, people didn't avoid their shadows.
Nor did they worship them.
They simply acknowledged them.

The sun's shadow walked alongside the body's.
The moon's shadow projected in dreams.

And at the center of it all,
the one who was both
watched.

Not because the shadow had disappeared,
but because it was no longer a separation.
It was part.

Epilogue – What Remains

The city was silent,
but it was not the silence of fear.
It was the silence of breath.

The walls no longer emitted light.
The streets no longer repeated commands.
And for the first time,
night fell without alarm.

The one who refuses to be erased stepped toward the center
of the Threshold, no longer hidden, but open at the heart of the
plaza.
There, she lit a filament lamp.
Not to illuminate.
But to remember.

In her hands, she held a notebook.
The oldest.
The most faithful.
"The one that recorded what all systems sought to erase."

And she read aloud—
not for the people,
not for the systems,
but for the shadows themselves:

"Light creates shadow.
And shadow, form.
One without the other is a lie.
Clarity without contrast is blindness.
Darkness without contour is emptiness.
Only when one curves within the other

does the true face of the world emerge.
And it is there, in that face, that we are finally seen."

The people did not applaud.
They did not fall silent.
They did not kneel.
They simply listened.
As one listens to a story that has always been known,
but until now, had never been told truthfully.

Then someone stepped forward to the whitest wall at the
center,
to cast their shadow.
The shadow of their body.
The shadow of their inner form.
And after them, others.
Silhouettes, movements, gestures.
Shadow after shadow.
Reflection after reflection.

Not as protest.
Not as worship.
As mirror.
As act.
As birth.

And then it was understood:
It was like returning a creation to its god
and kneeling not before its power, but before its magnificence:

The magnificence of the light of day and the light of night,
the shadow of the sun
and the shadow of the moon
in perfect balance.

A world where
the individual,
the light,
and the shadow
were no longer opposites,
but one.

And the city,
at last,
began to rebuild itself.

GLOSSARY OF LIGHT AND SHADOW

A symbolic lexicon for readers of **DESHADOWED.**

"Words fail to name what the shadow already knows."

Clarosoma™
A bio-optical harness designed to monitor and regulate physiological and emotional responses. Once a tool of obedience, later revealed as a fragment of lost memory.

Nulux
The central consciousness of light. Invisible, faceless, absolute. It regulates all **Clarosoma™** systems, until the day it fell silent and remembered.

The Threshold (El Umbral)
A physical and symbolic boundary between the world of control and the memory of what was. A place that must not only be crossed but brought back.

The Veiled (Los Velados)
Those who chose to retain margins. They move within forgotten tunnels, preserving the memory of deviation and resisting the radiant order.

Penumbra Nova
The illuminated capital. A city designed for complete surveillance and purity of light. Its perfection masks a history of erased truths.

Transparent Citizen
A person entirely synchronized with the light system—shadowless, thoughtless, calibrated. A model of submission, devoid of contradiction.

The Silent Eclipse
A moment when light paused, and shadows returned. Not a failure, but a call. Not darkness—but awakening.

The Oldest Notebook
A surviving artifact from the Inventor, written not in ink but in shadow. It contains what no structure dared to preserve: the unfiltered origin of the **Clarosoma™**.

Shadow
Not absence, but witness. Not rebellion, but reflection. A presence that once followed, now leads.

AUTHOR'S NOTE

Deshadowed was written in the space between clarity and contradiction. It is a story about light, but not about enlightenment—rather, about what light fears to touch: memory, doubt, and the personal interiority that resists being measured.

This novel was never meant to be a dystopia. It is a mirror turned inward. In its world, the technologies are imagined—but the silence, the control, and the longing for shadow are not.

The shadow, in these pages, is not evil. It is history. It is imagination. It is what remains when language becomes too clean and certainty too sharp.

Thank you for walking with me across the Threshold.

May you keep your light curved,
and your shadow alive.

R. M. Cepeda Hodge
One who observes, sketches, builds, writes... and remembers.

Embrace the skin like a second consciousness, its function is not to protect: it is to erase, Eliminate the personal shadow by means of extreme, calibrated, omnidirectional light. The shadow finds no angle where it can survive.

Follow us:

Instagram

CEPEDAHODGE_ATELIER

Comments & questions

$9.99
ISBN 979-8-218-79204-6
50999>

9 798218 792046

www.ingramcontent.com/pod-product-compliance
Lightning Source LLC
Chambersburg PA
CBHW072045170626

46811CB00008B/3165